From the
library
of

....

....

The Marvelous Toy

WORDS AND MUSIC BY
TOM PAXTON

ILLUSTRATED BY
STEVE COX

*To Jim &
Laura's
family!*

T Paxton

imagine!
a Peter Yarrow Book
New York
www.imaginebks.com

When I was just a wee little lad,
Full of health and joy,
My father homeward came one night,
And gave to me a toy.

A wonder to behold, it was,
With many colors bright,
And the moment I laid eyes on it
It became my heart's delight.

It went zip! when it moved
And bop! when it stopped
And whirr! when it stood still.
I never knew just what it was,
And I guess I never will.

A wonder to behold, it was,
With many colors bright,
And the moment I laid eyes on it
It became my heart's delight.

The first time that I picked it up,
I had a big surprise,
For right on its bottom were two big buttons
That looked like big, green eyes.

I first pushed one and then the other,
And then I twisted its lid,
And when I set it down again,
This is what it did:

It went zip! when it moved
And bop! when it stopped
And whirr! when it stood still.

I never knew just what it was,
And I guess I never will.

It first marched left and then marched right,
And then marched under a chair,
And when I looked where it had gone
It wasn't even there.

I started to cry and my daddy laughed,
For he knew that I would find,
When I turned around, my marvelous toy,
Chugging from behind.

It went zip! when it moved
And bop! when it stopped
And whirr! when it stood still.
I never knew just what it was,
And I guess I never will.

Well, the years have gone by too quickly, it seems—
I have my own little boy,
And yesterday I gave to him
My marvelous little toy.

His eyes nearly popped right out of his head;
He gave a squeal of glee.
Neither one of us knows just what it is
But he loves it just like me.

It went zip! when it moved
And bop! when it stopped
And whirr! when it stood still.

I never knew just what it was,
And I guess I never will.